Refugee Grant
For Children
CUSD

Elinda Who Danced In The Sky

AN ESTONIAN FOLKTALE

ADAPTED BY LYNN MORONEY
ILLUSTRATED BY VEG REISBERG

CHILDREN'S BOOK PRESS • SAN FRANCISCO, CALIFORNIA

Long ago in a land far to the north, Elinda was born from a tiny bird's egg. Her hair was as dark as a winter night and her eyes were as bright as a summer day. She was kind-hearted and loved by all.

Elinda's work was to direct the birds in their migrations. Warning the birds of the coming of the snows, she showed them the special sky path to the warm lands. In spring, when it was time for their return, she gently guided each bird along the great path.

Elinda cared for the birds as tenderly as a mother. Word of her beauty and kindness spread, and it surprised no one that when she reached the age to be wed, many suitors came to ask for her hand. But Elinda turned them all away.

One night the North Star came to call. He came riding in a crystal sleigh drawn by a single crystal horse. He bowed and said, "Elinda, please marry me. I would be a dependable husband and you would always know where to find me."

But Elinda thought, "North Star would always be distant and unmoving and I would have to stay in the same place all the time."

"North Star, I cannot marry you," she said.

Later, Moon came. He glided down from the sky in a chariot drawn by four silver horses. He bowed and said, "Elinda, please marry me. I would be a romantic husband. With me you could travel to a new place each night."

But Elinda thought, "Moon travels, but he always takes the same narrow path."

"Moon, I cannot marry you," replied Elinda.

Still later, Sun came down from the sky in a carriage of pure gold drawn by twelve gold horses. "Elinda," he said, "you must marry me. With me you will light the day. We will warm the winds and cause the seasons to come and go."

But Elinda thought, "Sun's light is too harsh. I would have to hide from his glare, always living in his shadow. My own light would never be seen."

"Sun, I cannot marry you." she said.

Then, towards midnight, the whole sky filled with shimmering lights. A gleaming black carriage descended from the sky, drawn by a hundred rainbow-colored horses. Inside rode Prince Borealis, Lord of the Northern Lights.

Elinda, please marry me," he said. "With me you will not remain fixed in one place, but come and go. You will not take a narrow path, but travel the whole sky. My light is not harsh, but gentle and soothing."

"Yes," said Elinda. "I will marry you."

Then, while the world was sleeping, Elinda and Prince Borealis danced across the night sky.

Finally, Prince Borealis said, "Soon day will come and I must return to my own land. Prepare for our wedding and I shall return at nightfall." With these words he faded into the dawn.

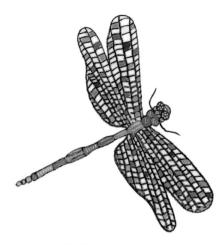

Elinda began to weave her wedding veil. With the help of the birds, she gathered the sparkle from the dew drops. The dragonflies gave her the iridescence from their wings. Under the watchful eyes of the spiders, she spun magic thread. Then, sitting at a golden loom, she began to weave a veil so delicate that it could scarcely be seen.

As night fell, Prince Borealis made preparations to return to his beloved Elinda. But the spirits of his own land refused to let him go, saying that he was needed by his own people.

When Prince Borealis did not return, Elinda continued her weaving. The veil soon filled the weaving room and spilled out into the countryside. Days turned into weeks, weeks into months, and the veil grew longer and longer. When at last the veil reached the end of the earth, Elinda rested her hands. Believing the prince would never return, she wept until her tears filled the rivers and streams of earth.

When Elinda lifted her head at last, she saw that the birds had been watching over her in her grief. At her bidding, they came together and gently carried her higher and higher, up into the sky. Then they crowned her with stars.

Elinda now reigns as queen of the sky. Once again she tends to the birds and directs them along the sky path. North Star is her constant friend; Moon leaves his path once a month to visit her; and Sun sends his warm greetings each day.

From time to time, in the deepest of winter, Elinda is once again seen dancing with the prince, although they never marry. As for Elinda's wedding veil, it may be seen on any clear night, drifting from one end of the sky to the other. It is called the Milky Way.

Elinda Who Danced In The Sky

This story comes from the Eastern European country of Estonia. The roots of the story are found in the "Song of Salme" in the epic poem of Estonia, *The Kalevipoeg.* Our sources include: H. Jannsen's *Marchen und Sagen Des Estinishchen Volkes* (Dorpat, 1881) and W.F. Kirby's *The Hero of Estonia* (London, 1895). In our retelling of the story we have been guided by the scholarship that identifies Elinda as an ancient sky goddess who would act on her own initiative, rather than allow herself to be carried up to the sky by her father—as in some 19th century versions of the story.

Oklahoma storyteller Lynn Moroney and San Francisco artist Veg Reisberg previously collaborated on *Baby Rattlesnake,* which *Publishers Weekly* called "A winning retelling of a Native American tale…. (with) vivid, fanciful illustrations." Veg Reisberg also did the paintings for *Uncle Nacho's Hat,* A Reading Rainbow Selection. Both *Baby Rattlesnake and Uncle Nacho's Hat* were published by Children's Book Press.

Text copyright © 1990 by Lynn Moroney. All rights reserved.
Illustrations copyright © 1990 by Veg Reisberg. All rights reserved.
Editors: Harriet Rohmer and David Schecter
Design: Armagh Cassil and Veg Reisberg, Somar Graphics
Production Assistant: Julie Weigel
Typography: Berna Alvarado-Rodriguez
Printed in Hong Kong through Interprint
Children's Book Press is a nonprofit community publisher.

Library of Congress Cataloging-in-Publication Data
Moroney, Lynn.
Elinda who danced in the sky: an Estonian folktale / adapted by Lynn Moroney; illustrated by Veg Reisberg.
   p. cm.
   Summary: An Estonian folktale about the sky goddess Elinda, who overcomes her disappointment at losing
Prince Borealis and continues her work of guiding the birds in their migrations.
   ISBN 0-89239-066-2 : $12.95
   [1. Sky—Folklore. 2. Folklore—Estonia.] I. Reisberg, Veg, ill. II. Title.
PZ8.1.M826E1 1990
398.21'0947'41—dc20   90-2247
                                                              CIP
                                                              AC

For Siobhan and Tracy. Thanks, also to: Dr. John Dunne, Dr. Felix Oinas, Dr. Cary Sneider, Gretchen Mayo, Robert Wilhelm, and the Oklahoma City librarians. (Lynn Moroney)

For my students at A.P. Giannini and Aptos schools. Thanks, also to: Claire Cotts, Glenn Hirsch, Heldi Valvur, Cynthia Lane, Laura White, Annee Boulanger, Victoria Kauffman, Joyce Harada, Theresa Hernenko, Ilya Les, Robert Irminger, Justine Perez, Roz Chang and Linda Perkins. (Veg Reisberg)